The Prince and the Perfect Pillow

Written by

Julie Kelly

Illustrated by

Jordan Sandy

There was once a prince who lived in a castle way up high. When he reached out of his window he could almost touch the sky.

2

3

He had all he ever wanted money, toys and sweets, but there was just one problem he found it hard to sleep.

Every night he tossed and turned and counted lots of sheep, but nothing seemed to work for him, and still he couldn't sleep.

"I hate this awful pillow" he would always say. "Go and find me something better, there no price that I won't pay."

So off his servants went on their way, to find the perfect pillow that would save the day.

They brought him pillows from all over the land some very strange, some very grand.

There was one filled with feathers that tickled his nose,
One filled with foam that just made him groan.

He tried one with lumps and bumps and one that wobbled like jelly,

The final one he'd had enough was just so awfully smelly.

Then one day in a place far far away his servants found a girl collecting hay. The girls' name was Little Bo Sleep and she worked all day looking after her sheep.

They told of the prince and his sad sad tale of how he'd no sleep and was looking quite pale. "I can help," Bo Sleep said "I will make the perfect pillow for his royal head."

She made the cover with such delight, by the magic of the moon at night. She filled it with wool from her finest sheep, soft and cosy for a good night sleep.

When it was ready she was happy as could be and took it to the prince for him to see.

"This is a gift from me, your perfect pillow just wait and see, you will sleep so heavenly."

That night he went to bed and lay down his sleepy head.

He dreamt he was floating on a cloud, soft and fluffy with love all around.

He woke as the light shone on a brand new day, he jumped up and down shouting hurry!

"At last I've slept all night, it's great to wake and feel so bright, so today to celebrate we'll have a party something great, food, cakes, and drinks for all, music and dancing in the hall".

He looked at Bo Sleep and smiled...
"And you will be my special guest, to thank you for the gift of rest, for your perfect pillow is the best!"

The Prince and the Perfect Pillow

Dedicated to

Shane & Ciara

Printed in Great Britain
by Amazon